Learning Resources Center
University of Wyoming Libraries.
Laramie, WY 82070

‹ GRENADA ›

PLACES AND PEOPLES OF THE WORLD
GRENADA

Joyce Eisenberg

CHELSEA HOUSE PUBLISHERS
New York • Philadelphia

COVER: A Grenadian man plays a drum in his walled backyard. Drumming is heard in neighborhoods throughout this island nation.

Editorial Director: Rebecca Stefoff
Editor: Bill Finan
Copy Editor: Crystal G. Norris
Art Director: Janice Engelke
Designer: Maureen McCafferty
Production Manager: Brian A. Shulik
Editorial Assistant: Daniel M. Wolpe
Photo Research: PAR/NYC

Copyright © 1988 by Chelsea House Publishers,
a division of Main Line Book Co. All rights reserved.

5 7 9 8 6

Library of Congress Cataloging-In-Publication Data

Eisenberg, Joyce.
Grenada.
Includes index.
Summary: Surveys the history, topography, people, and culture of Grenada, with emphasis on its current economy, industry, and place in the political world.
I. Grenada. [1. Grenada]
I. Title.
F2056.E37 1988 972.98'45 87-18274

ISBN 1-55546-777-6

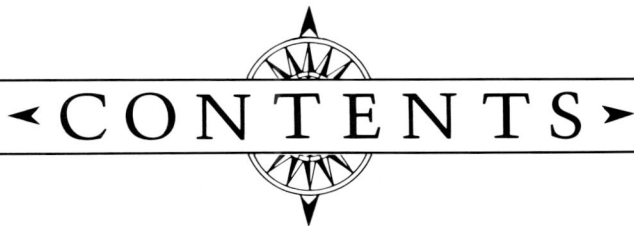

CONTENTS

Map 6
Facts at a Glance 9
History at a Glance 11
Chapter 1 Grenada and the World 15
Chapter 2 Land and Sea 19
Chapter 3 Past and Present 27
Chapter 4 The People of Grenada 39
          Color Section Scenes of Grenada 41
Chapter 5 Government and Education 55
Chapter 6 Economy and Communications 61
Chapter 7 Saint George's and Other Cities 69
Chapter 8 Arts and Culture 73
Chapter 9 Looking to the Future 79
Glossary 81
Index 85

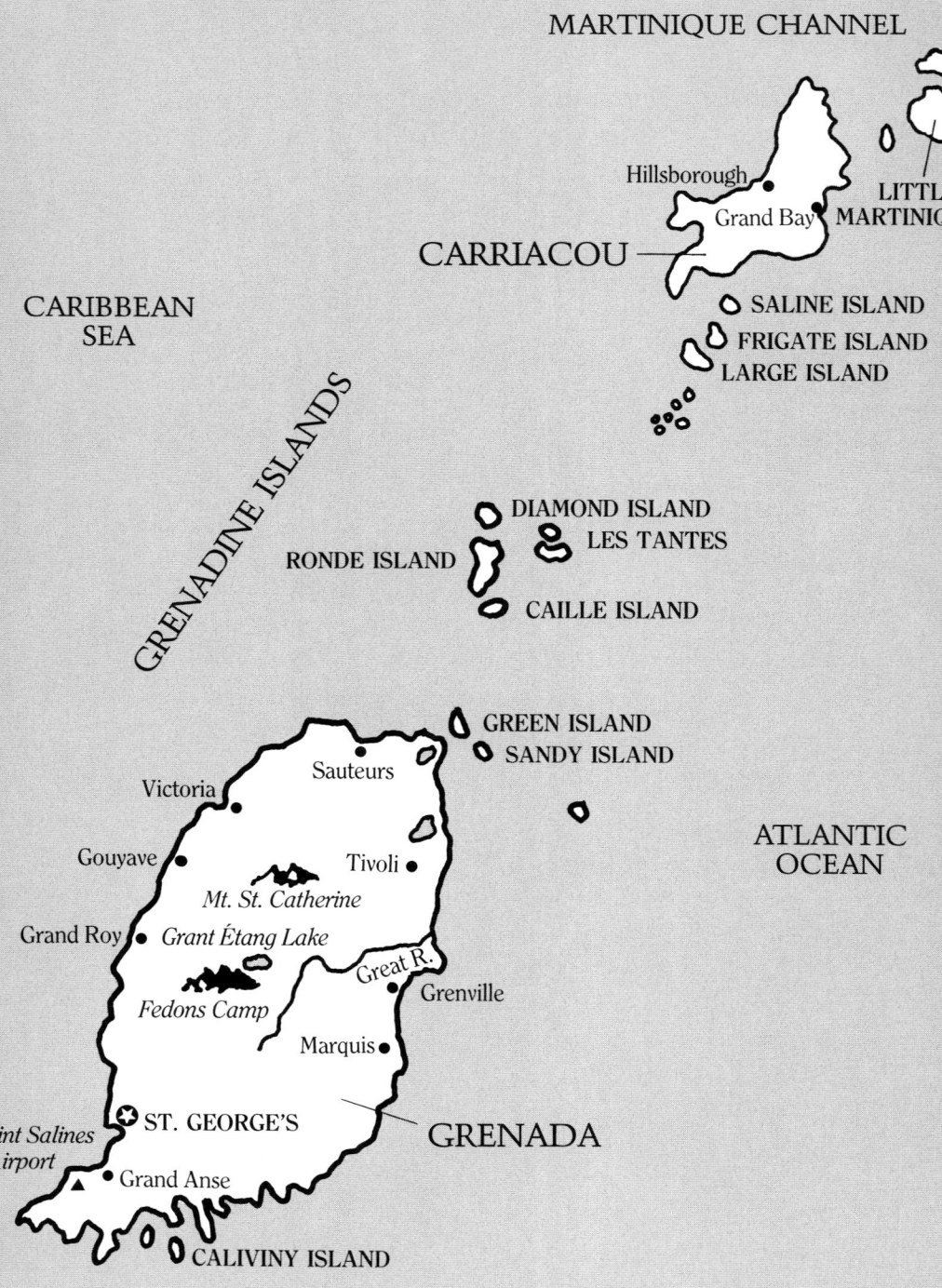

N

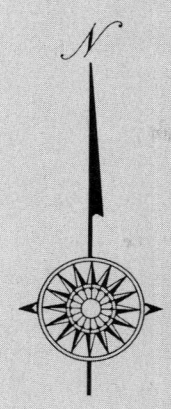

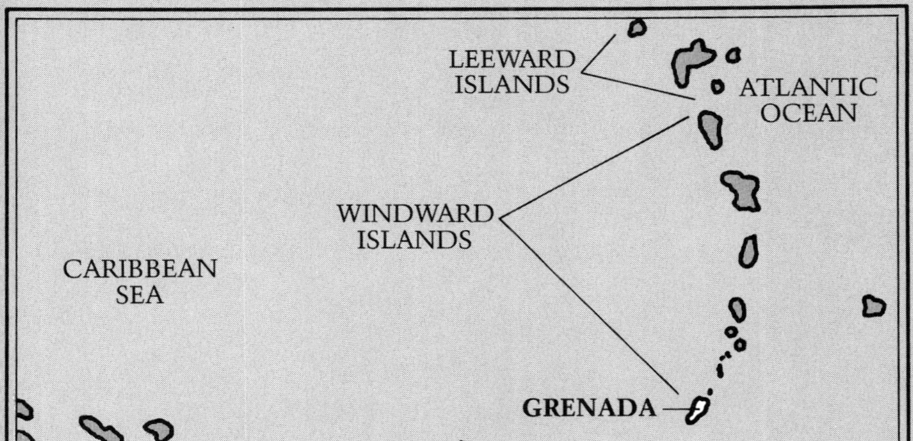
LEEWARD
ISLANDS
ATLANTIC
OCEAN
WINDWARD
ISLANDS
CARIBBEAN
SEA
GRENADA
SOUTH AMERICA

◄ FACTS AT A GLANCE ►

Land and People

Area	133 square miles (346 square kilometers)
Highest Point	Mount Saint Catherine, 2,757 feet (827 meters)
Coastline	75 miles (121 kilometers)
Greatest Length	21 miles (34 km)
Greatest Width	12 miles (19 km)
Major Lakes	Levera Pond, Lake Antoine, Grand Étang
Major Rivers	Duquesne, Little Saint Patrick, Black Bay
Capital	Saint George's (population 33,000)
Other Major Cities	Grenville (population 6,000), Gouyave (population 5,000), Sauteurs (population 3,000)
Population	100,000
Population Density	751 people per square mile (289 per sq km)
Official Language	English
Literacy Rate	85 percent
Major Ethnic Groups	Black or mulatto, 95 percent; East Indian or Asian, nearly 5 percent; white, less than 1 percent
Religions	Roman Catholic, Anglican, Methodist, Presbyterian, Seventh-Day Adventist, Baptist

Economy

Agriculture	35,000 acres (14,000 hectares) of land are under cultivation
Chief Crops	Nutmeg, cocoa, and bananas
Exports	Nutmeg, cocoa, and bananas, 90 percent of total; cinnamon, bay leaves, saffron, cloves, allspice, coconuts, limes, arrowroot, sugar, and cotton, 10 percent
Industry	Tourism accounts for 40 percent of the total national product; Grenada hosts about 38,000 people each year
Employment statistics	Unemployment, 35 to 40 percent; 43 percent of the total population is employed as follows: government and other services, 44 percent; agriculture, 40 percent; construction, manufacturing, and tourism, 16 percent
Currency	Eastern Caribbean dollar, divided into 100 cents
Gross Domestic Product	Equal to U.S. $940 per person per year
United States Aid	$300 per person per year

Government

Form of Government	Democratic self-government within the Commonwealth of Nations (formerly the British Commonwealth)
Formal Head of State	The British monarch, represented by the governor-general
Head of Government	Prime minister, elected by members of the House of Representatives to a five-year term
Cabinet	Six ministers appointed by the prime minister
Parliament	A House of Representatives with 15 elected members, and a Senate with 13 members appointed by the ruling party and the opposition party

HISTORY AT A GLANCE

by 4000 B.C.	The Ciboney Indians, native to South America, establish themselves on Grenada. Later, the Arawak Indians settle the island.
1000 to 1300 A.D.	The warlike Carib Indians arrive on the island, which they name Camerhogne. They kill or enslave the Arawaks.
1498	During his third voyage to the New World, Christopher Columbus sights the island and names it Concepción. His sailors call it Granada.
1609	London merchants attempt to found a settlement on the island but are defeated by the Carib Indians.
1650	The French buy the island from the Caribs, who later try unsuccessfully to recapture it.
1657	The French governor of Martinique sells the island to Comte Jean Faudoas de Cerrillac.
1674	Renamed La Grenade, the island officially becomes a French colony.
1700s	The British and French struggle for control of the Caribbean Islands, including Grenada. The French build Fort Rupert in 1705. They also begin Fort Frederick. African slaves are brought in to work in the sugarcane plantations.
1762	England wins sovereignty over the island and renames it Grenada.
1779	Led by Comte d'Estaing, French forces regain control of the island.

1783	Under the Treaty of Versailles, France returns Grenada to British rule. The British complete Fort Frederick.
1795	Julien Fedon, a black planter, leads an unsuccessful revolt against British rule.
1834	The Emancipation Act abolishes slavery on the island.
1877	Grenada officially becomes a British colony.
1940s	Labor and independence movements gain strength throughout the West Indies.
1955	Hurricane Janet strikes the island, killing 137 Grenadians and destroying the nutmeg and cocoa crops.
1958 to 1962	Grenada is a member of the ten-nation Federation of the West Indies.
1967	As a member of the West Indian Associated States, Grenada receives self-government for internal affairs. Great Britain is responsible for defense and foreign affairs.
early 1970s	Island politicians are divided on the issue of independence from Great Britain.
1974	Grenada receives total independence. Eric Gairy, head of the Grenada United Labor party, is named prime minister. Sir Paul Scoon is governor-general.
1979	Maurice Bishop and other members of the New Jewel Movement overthrow Gairy's government and proclaim a People's Revolutionary Government. Bishop becomes prime minister. He develops ties with Cuba and other Communist nations.
early 1980s	Grenada's relationship with the United States deteriorates as its ties with Cuba grow stronger.
1983	Bernard Coard and Hudson Austin overthrow Bishop. A riot in the capital results in 100 deaths. Bishop and some members of his regime are executed. Austin sets up the Revolutionary Military Council.

October 1983	Caribbean soldiers, led by United States troops, invade Grenada. After three days of fighting, the invasion force defeats Cuban and Grenadian soldiers and controls the island. Sir Paul Scoon assumes control of the government.
1984	In the first free elections since 1976, Herbert Blaize is elected prime minister and the New National party comes to power.
1985	The last United States soldiers leave Grenada.

A young girl and her brother pump water from an outside well. Their tin-roofed home is similar to many Grenadian houses in rural areas.

Grenada and the World

Grenada (pronounced "Gruh-NAY-duh") is one of the smallest independent nations in the Western Hemisphere. Bordered on its west coast by the Caribbean Sea and on the east coast by the Atlantic Ocean, Grenada lies at the southern end of the Windward island chain, about 90 miles (145 kilometers) north of Venezuela. With its dependencies—the nearby islands of Carriacou (the largest of the Grenadine Islands) and Petit Martinique—the country's area is 133 square miles (346 square kilometers).

Sometimes called the "Isle of Spice," Grenada is the only spice-producer in the Western Hemisphere, with more spices per square mile (2.6 square kilometers) than any other country in the world. Throughout this fertile, tropical island, the air is fragrant with cinnamon, nutmeg, and cloves. Grenada grows one-third of the world's supply of nutmeg, and this export is so important to Grenada's economy that the national flag has a picture of nutmeg on it.

Considered one of the most beautiful islands in the West Indies, Grenada boasts lofty mountains, lush rain forests, deep valleys, white, sandy beaches, and sheltered harbors. Its year-round mild temperatures, fine beaches, and warm seas have made the island a port of call for many cruise ships. Tourism plays a vital role in Grenada's economy.

Approximately 95 percent of Grenada's 100,000 residents are black or of mixed race—the descendants of African slaves who worked the island's sugarcane plantations during the 18th century. More than half of the islanders are Roman Catholic. White and East Indian minorities make up the rest of the population.

Grenada's bountiful spices and sugarcane made it a prize for European adventurers. The island was discovered by Christopher Columbus in 1498; in 1609, the British tried to colonize it but were held off by the Carib Indians, the native inhabitants of the Caribbean region.

During the next 150 years, possession of the island shifted between France and Great Britain. Both countries imported large numbers of African slaves to work the sugarcane plantations. In 1783, Grenada became a British colony, and it remained under British control until its indepen-

An 18th-century cannon stands as a reminder of the battles fought by the British and the French to control Grenada and its surrounding islands.

dence in 1974. During the years of British rule, slavery was abolished and many Grenadians became landowners.

The first ten years after independence were as unsettled as the centuries before. In 1979, the government of Prime Minister Sir Eric Gairy was overthrown by the New Jewel Movement, a Marxist group led by Maurice Bishop that sought economic and technical assistance from Cuba and the Soviet Union. The Cubans sent money and technicians to build an international airport at Point Salines and then stored a large quantity of military equipment there.

Deep divisions grew within Bishop's party, and in 1983 Deputy Prime Minister Bernard Coard, apparently favoring ties with the Soviet Union, led another coup in which Bishop was assassinated along with four other government leaders. About 100 civilians were killed during the uprising. Alarmed by these events, the Organization of Eastern Caribbean States—an organization of five nations formed in 1981—requested that the United States try to resolve the situation. On October 25, 1983, President Ronald Reagan ordered about 1,900 U.S. soldiers onto the island. They were accompanied by several hundred troops from neighboring Caribbean islands.

Order was restored, and a nonpolitical interim administration led by Governor-General Sir Paul Scoon oversaw island affairs until 1984, when democratic elections were held. Today, Grenada remains a member of the Commonwealth of Nations, an association of independent states—most of them former British colonies—that recognize the British monarch.

Although tourism declined during the recent political unrest, it has been revitalized since the government was stabilized. In addition, a new airport able to handle large aircraft was completed, and it has made it easier for tourists to visit the Caribbean's Isle of Spice.

Waterfalls are found throughout this mountainous island. The Concord Falls pictured above flow into the Black Bay River in northern Grenada.

Land and Sea

The island of Grenada, in the Eastern Caribbean, is part of the West Indies, a chain of islands formed by the peaks of the Caribbean Andes, a partially submerged mountain chain that once connected North and South America. This island chain, which divides the Atlantic Ocean and the Caribbean Sea, forms a 2,500-mile (4,025-kilometer) arc that stretches from Cuba, 50 miles (80 km) off the tip of Florida, to Trinidad, near Venezuela. Two major West Indian island groups, the Greater Antilles and the Lesser Antilles, lie in the region south of the Bahamas. Grenada belongs to the Lesser Antilles.

The Lesser Antilles extend from the Virgin Islands in the north to Grenada in the south. The northern part of the chain is known as the Leeward Islands. The southern part, which includes Grenada, is called the Windward Islands. The Windward Islands are more exposed than are the Leeward Islands to the constant trade winds that blow from northeast to southwest.

Grenada's closest island neighbors are Saint Vincent, 65 miles (105 kilometers) north; Barbados, 150 miles (241 km) northeast; and Trinidad, 90 miles (145 km) south.

The main island is 21 miles (34 kilometers) long and 12 miles (19 km) wide at its widest point—about twice the size of Washington, D.C. At the northern end of the island is Sauteurs Bay; at the southwest is the beach-bordered peninsula called Point Salines, the site of the new international airport.

Grenada has an astounding variety of terrain, including tall mountains covered with rain forests, deserts where only cacti thrive, racing rivers and streams, deep valleys, cascading waterfalls, clear lakes, a string of white-and-black sand beaches, and picturesque harbors.

The island was formed by volcanic eruptions millions of years ago. Today, the extinct volcanoes' craters are filled with lakes, including Levera Pond and Lake Antoine in the northeast and Grand Étang Lake in the center of the island. Surrounding glasslike, cobalt-blue Grand Étang Lake is a forest reserve, with monkeys, armadillos, a bird sanctuary, and hundreds of varieties of orchids.

Grenada's landscape ranges from towering, rain-forest-covered mountains to white sandy beaches shaded by palm trees.

A mountain range covered with tropical rain forest runs north-to-south through the center of Grenada, dividing the island in half. Mount Saint Catherine, 2,757 feet (827 meters) tall, is the highest point on the island. The peaks of Mount Granby, Mount Lebanon, and Mount Sinai reach heights of more than 2,000 feet (600 m).

Although stretches of desert and cactus extend southwest of the mountain range, the coastal land to the southeast and northwest is very fertile. This is Grenada's prime agricultural region, where spices, bananas, and many kinds of fruits and vegetables grow. Between Grand Étang Lake and Grenville, a city halfway up the east coast, runs the fertile Great River Valley. The valley of Saint John's River runs between the lake and Saint George's, the capital city on the west coast. In the northwest, valleys surround the Duquesne and Little Saint Patrick rivers. The waters of the

Concord Waterfall run into the Black Bay River and tumble down the Concord Valley. Not far from Saint George's is the beautiful Annandale Falls, where mountain streams cascade 50 feet (15 meters) into a crystal, freshwater pool surrounded by tropical plants.

After agriculture, tourism is the second major economic activity in Grenada. Along the country's 80 miles (129 kilometers) of coast are more than 65 bays and 45 white-sand beaches. The bays offer the world's best sailing, and the beaches attract sun worshippers. The water is almost always inviting; its average temperature is about 80° Fahrenheit (26° Centigrade). Along the Caribbean (west) coast, the sand beaches are fronted by calm, clear water—so clear that tropical fish and 40 species of coral are visible 200 feet (60 meters) from shore.

Two of the island's most spectacular Caribbean beaches are located on the southern tip of the island: L'Anse aux Épines (Beach of Pines) and Grand Anse, a 2-mile (3.2-kilometer) crescent of sand that ends in a palm-covered point. Not surprisingly, this is the heart of the resort area.

In contrast, on Grenada's east coast, a heavy Atlantic surf pounds against uninhabited beaches. Notable features of this coast are Bacolet Bay, a wild peninsula that juts into the Atlantic south of Grenville, and Levera Bay, the meeting place of the Caribbean Sea and the Atlantic Ocean at the island's northeastern tip. From here, the first island of the Grenadines chain is visible, curving north from Levera Bay. Levera Beach is a deserted stretch of sand ringed by sea grapes and palm trees.

Tiny islands surround Grenada. Just off the shore of Levera Beach are Sugar Loaf, Sandy Island, and Green Island, which are frequented by sailing enthusiasts. Off Grenada's southwest tip is Glover Island. To the east, in Clarkes Court Bay, are Calivigny Island and Hog Island. Fishermen and snorkelers are the chief visitors to these three uninhabited islands.

The Grenadines

The nation of Grenada also includes some inhabited islands from the Grenadines chain, an archipelago of 8 larger and more than 120 smaller islands that curves north from Grenada to Saint Vincent. Carriacou, about 16 miles (26 kilometers) north of Grenada, is the largest of the Grenadines, with 13 square miles (34 square kilometers) of rolling hills and sandy beaches. Petit Martinique, about 3 miles (4.8 km) northeast of Carriacou, is just 464 acres (186 hectares) in area. A handful of the picturesque smaller islands, such as Ronde Island, belong to Grenada. The rest of the Grenadines are under the jurisdiction of Saint Vincent.

Carriacou's colonial history parallels Grenada's. Most of the 7,000 islanders are descendants of African slaves, many of whom can trace their ancestry to a particular African tribe. Because the island is so isolated, the people have maintained many traditional cultural and spiritual traditions. A small number of islanders of Scottish descent hand-build some of the Caribbean's finest sailing boats.

The island's picturesque coastline features a series of sheltered natural harbors and sandy beaches, fertile coastal flatlands, and a central ridge of hills sloping up from the sea. The chain of hills, which runs from Gun Point in the north to the protected harbor of Tyrrel Bay in the south, culminates in the 675-foot (203-meter) peaks of Belle Vue North and Belle Vue South, known locally as High North and Capeau Garre.

Hillsborough, the island's only major town, has about 580 residents; it is the capital city and main port of entry, with about 580 residents. The post office, banks, and small shops are located here. Market day is on Monday, when the produce arrives from Grenada; on Saturday, the mail boat arrives. A senior executive officer, supervised by a parliamentary secretary, administers the affairs of both Carriacou and Petit Martinique from an office in Hillsborough. Nearby, the Carriacou Museum exhibits American Indian and European artifacts reflecting the island's history.

Ruins of great houses in the hills testify that Carriacou was once a prosperous, sugar-growing island. The old sugarcane fields are now used to grow cotton, peanuts, and limes. Because the soil is poor, the crops meet only local needs. Tourism brings in some money; the island is known internationally for good sailing.

Fishermen rest against their boats after a day of fishing off Carriacou.

Tyrrel Bay, a shipbuilding center on the west coast, is one of the finest natural harbors in the West Indies. The beach is cluttered with boats in various stages of construction, being readied for the West Indian trade schooner fleet.

Petit Martinique was settled by the French; today, about 700 islanders of French descent live on the tiny island year-round. Like the inhabitants of Carriacou, most of the people are employed in shipbuilding and seamanship. There are few accommodations for visitors, and islanders must take the ferry to travel to and from Carriacou.

Climate

Grenada's climate is tropical, tempered by trade winds. The average temperature is 82° Fahrenheit (28° Centigrade); throughout the year, the temperature varies little, usually fewer than 5° F (3° C). But in the mountains around Grand Étang Lake, the temperature can be as much as 10° F (6° C) cooler than along the coast.

The dry winter season runs from December to May, and the rainy summer season from June to November. Even during the rainy season, the weather may be sunny for days at a stretch. When it does rain, a cloudburst usually lasts from a few minutes to a half-hour before the sun reappears. Although Grenada is not in the hurricane belt, it was hard hit in 1955 by Hurricane Janet, which left 137 people dead and destroyed most of the island's cacao and nutmeg trees.

On the northeast (windward) side of the island, the trade winds bring an average annual rainfall of more than 200 inches (5,080 millimeters). On the sheltered southwest (leeward) side, the average rainfall is much less—about 60 inches (1,524 mm) a year. June is the wettest month, with an average of 12 inches (305 mm) of rain. March is the driest month, averaging 1 inch (25.4 mm) of rain. The driest region of Grenada is the south, where the tourist hotels are located. The wettest, highest, and coolest section is the central forests.

This 16th-century engraving captures early European explorers' impressions of life in West Indian islands such as Grenada.

Past and Present

Ancient rock carvings discovered on Grenada reveal that the original settlers were a tribe of South American Indians called Ciboneys, who lived on the island as early as 4000 B.C. Centuries later, the peace-loving Arawak Indians arrived, but later they were enslaved or killed by the fierce, cannibalistic Carib Indians, who traveled by canoe from South America to the Caribbean sometime between 1000 and 1300 A.D. The Caribs named the island Camerhogne.

On August 15, 1498, during his third voyage to the New World, Christopher Columbus discovered the island, although he did not land on it. He named the island Concepción, but the Spanish sailors on his ship called it Granada because it reminded them of that green-hilled Spanish city.

In search of spices, Columbus hoped to find a short sea route to India by sailing west across the Atlantic Ocean instead of east on the time-consuming and expensive journey around Africa's Cape Horn. It is ironic that Columbus never explored Grenada. Of all the Caribbean islands he visited, it was the only one that could have fulfilled his original goal by opening up a new source of spices for Europe.

In 1609, London merchants tried to establish a settlement on the island, but the Caribs easily defeated them. In 1650, the French succeeded in setting up a colony after a series of bloody skirmishes. They were led by

Marie Bonnard du Parquet, governor of the nearby island of Martinique, who persuaded the Indians to sell the island for some knives and hatchets, a large quantity of glass beads, and two bottles of brandy for the chief. Nine months later, the Caribs began a futile struggle to recapture the island from the French.

In the following decades, the British and French traded ownership of the island several times. In 1657, du Parquet sold the island to Comte Jean Faudoas de Cerrillac. In 1674, it became a French colony called La Grenade. But in 1762, the British took the island from the French, who formally gave it to Great Britain under the Treaty of Paris on February 10, 1763. The British named the island Grenada, as it is known today.

This tug-of-war between France and Britain occurred on many islands of the Lesser Antilles, where the sugarcane crop was tremendously profitable. On Grenada, the two nations amassed troops at opposite ends of the island, built substantial fortifications, and battled stubbornly for decades. As a legacy of this era, Grenada's capital, Saint George's, is flanked by two historic landmarks: Fort Rupert, built by the French in 1705, and Fort Frederick, begun by the French and completed by the British in 1783.

In 1779, the French regained control of the island, but gave it again to the British in 1783 under the Treaty of Versailles. The British controlled Grenada, first as a territory and then as a formal colony, until the island became an independent nation in 1974.

During the 18th century, both the British and the French imported black slaves from Africa to work the cotton, coffee, and sugarcane plantations. In 1795, Julien Fedon, a black planter inspired by the ideas of the French Revolution, led a bloody revolt against the British. Sir Ralph Abercromby suppressed the uprising—but not until one-fourth of the island's slave population had either died or disappeared.

Slave uprisings, provoked by the French who had remained on the island, plagued the government until 1834, when the British Parliament passed the Emancipation Act, which abolished slavery in the British empire. Many former slaves emigrated to Trinidad, which offered better

African slaves were brought to Grenada to work on colonial sugar plantations.

working conditions, or settled in the interior of Grenada. With no slaves to work the plantations, sugarcane profits declined drastically. The British tried unsuccessfully to bring in large numbers of Indian and Malayan indentured laborers. In 1877, Grenada officially became a British colony.

Independence

From 1900 to 1945, West Indians throughout the Caribbean islands created a strong labor movement. Sugar harvesters in Saint Kitts, coal heavers in Saint Lucia, and workers in the Trinidad oilfields struck for better wages and working conditions. Between 1937 and 1957, the West Indian labor movement grew faster than the labor movement in the United States.

Alarmed by violent riots on Jamaican sugar plantations during 1937 and 1938, the British government sent a commission to the islands to investigate the causes of unrest and to make recommendations. The commission's report, written during World War II but not published until 1945, spelled out the need for reform and labor legislation. As West Indian labor leaders emerged, the trade union movement became an effective political force. The main goal of labor leaders during the 1940s was self-government for the islands. These leaders believed that self-rule would pave the way for a better standard of living and, ultimately, for independence.

In 1958, Grenada joined the newly formed Federation of the West Indies, which included Jamaica, Barbados, the Windward Islands, the Leeward Islands, and Trinidad and Tobago. This ten-nation federation hoped to establish a common regional government that would be independent of Great Britain. But the great physical distances between the islands, inadequate communications systems, and disagreement over what form this new government should take led to the federation's collapse in 1962.

In 1967, the island entered into a new relationship with Britain as one of the West Indies Associated States, which included Antigua, Dominica, and Saint Vincent, among others. The governments of these territories were responsible for domestic affairs, while Britain remained in charge of defense and external affairs. Any individual state could end the association by a decision of its legislative council and a popular vote.

During the early 1970s, Grenadian politics became divided between people who wanted independence from Great Britain and those who did not. On February 7, 1974, Grenada became an independent nation and a sovereign state within the British Commonwealth. Sir Paul Scoon, a Grenadian knighted by Britain, represented the queen in the largely ceremonial post of governor-general.

Eric Gairy, the first prime minister, quickly became an autocratic ruler.

The island's first prime minister after independence was Eric Gairy, the head of Grenada's United Labour party. He had dominated island politics since the early 1950s. Despite his early support for the workers, Gairy's administration was not a triumph of democracy. His opponents claimed that he went into political office bankrupt, owing money to many, but within three years he had enough money to buy several buildings. The Mongoose Gang, a secret police unit, bullied Gairy's critics and political opponents, many of whom were jailed.

Gairy was best known outside Grenada for his passionate speeches about unidentified flying objects at the United Nations. He claimed to possess mystical powers (he once supposedly "walked on water" in public) and was widely believed to practice *obeah* (witchcraft).

Gairy and his supporters were constantly at odds with a Socialist political party known as the New Jewel Movement (NJM), formed in 1973 by Maurice Bishop, a 28-year-old London-trained lawyer. The NJM mounted street protests and contested Gairy's policies. As a result, the Mongoose Gang cracked down. On November 18, 1973, a day that came to be known as Bloody Sunday, Bishop and five other NJM leaders were beaten and thrown into prison. (They were later released.) Two months later, on Bloody Monday, Gairy's police shot and killed Rupert Bishop, Maurice's father, during street demonstrations.

This oppression strengthened the NJM. When rumors reached Bishop and his supporters that Gairy was going to arrest them again, they decided to act quickly. On March 13, 1979, while Gairy was in New York City, Bishop and other members of the NJM staged a revolt. Forty armed men seized an army barracks and the island's only radio station, from which they broadcast appeals to Grenadians to join their revolution. Thousands descended on police stations with crude weapons.

In 12 hours, Gairy's regime had ended. Three people were killed during the takeover, the first revolution to overthrow an independent government in the English-speaking Caribbean. Bishop and his party established the People's Revolutionary Government of Grenada, and Bishop became the island's second prime minister. But the revolution did not establish democracy in Grenada.

Bishop's new regime, called the People's Revolutionary Government, held Marxist views on how to govern, advocating leadership by the workers with the eventual goal of a classless society. But Bishop took a practical approach to solving Grenada's problems. Politically, he had been inspired by the traditions of Caribbean populism, which stressed social justice, independence for each national group, and grass-roots participation in politics by the people. He also drew on the ideas of the Black Power movement, a group formed by black Americans in the late 1960s to promote black leadership in politics and cultural life.

Grenada's revolutionary government established diplomatic relations with Communist Cuba. Cuba assisted the new government with military training and provided teachers, doctors, and other technicians.

Many Grenadians may not have been attracted to the revolution's ideology, but they probably welcomed Gairy's removal. They were pleased with the social improvements Bishop made. Often financed by Cuba and other countries linked to the Soviet Union, these improvements included free secondary education, a higher literacy rate, and more university scholarships. The government opened free medical clinics in the countryside and distributed free milk and other foods. It also built 45 miles (73 kilometers) of roads and improved the water and power systems.

But many Grenadians resented the government's violations of human rights. Elections were promised but never held. Three newspapers were shut down, and political opponents of the People's Revolutionary Government were imprisoned. Grenadians were required to attend "worker-education" classes, where government officials lectured people on how they should support the government's policies.

Bishop's revolution also caused concern among the leaders of neighboring Caribbean nations, who knew that shipments of arms and advisers had arrived from Cuba. The island's new educational and military programs were patterned after Cuba's.

After the 1979 revolt, United States president Jimmy Carter told Bishop that his government could not expect more economic aid from the United States if it developed close relations with Cuba. When President Ronald Reagan took office in 1981, he warned Bishop that his ties to Cuba posed a threat to the peace of the region. Relations with the United States continued to sour, while Grenada's links to the Soviet Union became stronger. The war of words between Reagan and Bishop escalated when Bishop announced that Cuban president Fidel Castro would help build an international airport at Point Salines, on the southwestern end of Grenada. This airport was a sore subject in Grenada.

For 25 years, Grenadians had wanted a first-class international airport to replace the tiny Pearls Airport. They hoped a new airport at Point Salines, which was near most of the hotels, would attract more tourists. Crops could be shipped more easily, too.

Grenada had asked the United States and Canada for help with the airport; both drew up plans, but took no action. As one of its first gestures of goodwill to Bishop's government, Cuba agreed to build the airport. The United States said it was concerned that the new airport would allow Cuba to watch over shipments of oil and other items from South American refineries to the United States. It was also worried that Grenada might allow Cuba or the Soviet Union to use the completed airport for military aircraft.

Recognizing the growing antagonism between the United States and Grenada, Bishop met with government officials in the U.S. to discuss their concerns. Back home, he talked of improving relations with the United States. Some members of his party resented this approach, and a serious disagreement developed. A strongly Marxist group led by Bernard Coard, Bishop's deputy prime minister, demanded joint leadership of the party. Bishop refused.

Bishop's moderate political approach may have been his undoing. On October 13, 1983, Coard and his supporters stripped Bishop of his powers and placed him under house arrest. Some people believe that Cuba

Supporters of Prime Minister Bishop flee Fort Rupert as a Soviet-made tank moves into position behind them.

encouraged Coard to remove Bishop from power. Others said that the rift was a personal power struggle, not a matter of political beliefs. Whatever the reasons, Coard and Commander General Hudson Austin of the army took over the government.

But Coard and Austin underestimated Bishop's popularity. On October 19, 10,000 to 25,000 Grenadians, many of them schoolchildren released from school by followers of Bishop, climbed the hills above the harbor in Saint George's and rushed the gates of Bishop's residence. Setting free their leader, the crowd surged through city streets, protesting his overthrow. Bishop spoke at a rally in the city's Market Square before the crowd marched on the army administrative headquarters at Fort Rupert. Suddenly, a Soviet-built, mud-colored armored personnel carrier pointed its machine gun at the crowd and randomly opened fire. As many as 100 people were killed. Their bodies were later taken away by soldiers and burned.

The soldiers recaptured Bishop and then shot him, along with two other ministers and two trade union leaders. Also executed was Education Minister Jacqueline Creft, the mother of Bishop's four-year-old son Vladimir. This day—October 19, 1983—became known as Bloody Wednesday.

General Austin, a former prison guard, announced that he was the new leader of a 16-man military government, the Revolutionary Military Council. He imposed a 24-hour curfew and warned that violators would be shot on sight. He banned demonstrations and closed schools and most businesses. But Coard and Austin were not truly in control of the island. Their coup had turned many Grenadians against the New Jewel Movement's revolution. It also soured them on Cuba, since many believed that the Cubans, despite Castro's apparent fondness for Bishop, had been behind Bishop's arrest and execution.

United States Intervention

On October 21, leaders of the other island nations belonging to the Organization of Eastern Caribbean States (Antigua, Dominica, Saint Lucia, Saint Kitts-Nevis, Montserrat, and Saint Vincent) requested assistance from Barbados, Jamaica, and the United States to restore order and democracy in Grenada. The leaders said they were worried by the "unprecedented threat to the peace and security of the region created by the vacuum of authority in Grenada." They were afraid the violent changes on the island would encourage revolutionaries in their own countries.

Marines from the U.S. invasion force patrol the streets of Grenville.

On October 25, 1983, Caribbean soldiers, led by 1,900 U.S. troops, invaded Grenada in Operation Urgent Fury. The United States's official reason for the invasion was to protect the lives of 1,000 Americans who were trapped on the island after the coup. But the Reagan administration also said that the Soviet-Cuban military buildup on Grenada was becoming a threat to U.S. strategic interests in the Caribbean.

The American troops took charge of Government House, where Governor-General Sir Paul Scoon had been under virtual house arrest. The 600 American students who attended Saint George's University School of Medicine were airlifted to the United States. Outnumbered and outgunned, the Grenadian army and Cuban militiamen on the island quickly surrendered.

By October 28, the invasion forces controlled the island. Coard, Austin, and their co-conspirators were taken into custody to await trial at Richmond Hill Prison. Eighteen U.S. soldiers were killed and 116 were wounded in the invasion. Twenty-four Cubans and 45 Grenadians were killed.

The U.S. invasion, which Grenadians refer to as "the rescue," was controversial. Many nations officially condemned it, but it was greeted with

Herbert Blaize was elected prime minister in the 1984 general election.

almost unanimous support throughout the Caribbean (with the exception of Cuba).

After the intervention, Governor-General Sir Paul Scoon became a one-man government. He severed diplomatic ties with the Soviet Union and Libya and allowed the Cubans to retain only one diplomat on the island. Scoon appointed a nine-member advisory council made up of Grenadian citizens, with Nicholas Braithwaite as chairman, to assist him until new general elections could be held. A 396-man peacekeeping force, including soldiers and police from neighboring islands, was in charge of policing the island.

The United States left behind some military personnel until June 1985, when the last soldiers left the island. But its financial presence remained strong. It sent Grenada $3.4 million in disaster relief and $50 million in long-term economic aid after the invasion. Tons of American construction supplies and equipment were flown to the island, where U.S. Army engineers supervised the rebuilding of roads, schools, water systems, and telephone and power facilities. The United States also helped Grenada complete its international airport at long last.

General elections were held December 3, 1984. They were the first free elections since 1976. Eighty-five percent of the island's 48,000 voters lined up to choose a 15-member National Assembly and a new prime minister.

The New National party received 59 percent of the vote and won 14 of the 15 seats in the new House of Representatives. Herbert Blaize, the leader of the New National party, was elected to a five-year term as prime minister. Blaize's party said it would work toward economic development and create safeguards against the abuse of power.

Almost all of Grenada's population is descended from African slaves who were brought to the country in the 18th century.

The People of Grenada

About 95 percent of Grenadians are descendants of the African slaves whom the French and British brought to the island to work the sugar plantations. Most are Roman Catholic, a legacy of the French rule, although many adopted the Protestant religions of their British rulers. Roman Catholic, Anglican, Methodist, Presbyterian, Seventh-Day Adventist, Baptist, and other religious groups maintain churches in the capital and in the smaller villages.

About 5 percent of the islanders are of East Indian origin, descendants of indentured laborers brought from India in the 19th century. Most of these practice the Hindu religion. The 1,000 or so whites on the island are mostly of Western European origin and belong to Protestant denominations. Few of the native American Indians remain, although the 1960 census recorded nine Caribs.

For almost 100 years, Grenada was a British colony. English remains the official language and is spoken everywhere, but with a distinctive Caribbean lilt. Grenadians also chat among themselves in their own patois—a local dialect composed mostly of French with some African words and rhythms mixed in. Frequently described as gentle, independent, and outspoken, Grenadians show unfailing hospitality and friendliness. At the entrance of Saint George's harbor stands *Christ of the Deep,* a statue given to the islanders by the Costa Cruise Line in remembrance of the hospitality Grenadians showed its passengers and crew when one of its ships burned in the harbor in 1961.

Grenadians are slightly old-fashioned, a trait that is perhaps a holdover from colonial days. For example, many find skimpy dress on downtown streets improper. The British left their mark in other ways. Driving is on the left side of the street, and many families still enjoy afternoon tea, complete with home-baked cakes and brown-sugar-sweetened tea served in English porcelain pots.

There are still reminders of French rule, too. Most of the place names are French, such as Grand Anse Bay, Morne Rouge, Sans Souci, and L'Anse aux Épines.

Daily Life

After the British abolished slavery in 1834, the sugar plantations on Grenada were broken up, and the land—and the income from it—was divided among the people. Newly freed slaves were given their own plots to farm. As a result, about 70 percent of Grenada's families today are landowners who own farms that are 2 acres (.8 hectare) or smaller in size.

Because the land and sea are so rich, few people go hungry. Although there is some poverty, it is not the oppressive, desperate poverty that haunts some other Caribbean islands. Signs of severe poverty, such as shantytowns, are scarce. Most islanders live in well-kept, brightly painted wooden houses. In the poorer villages, two-room cottages may have only tin roofs and cardboard walls.

The central market squares in Saint George's and Grenville are the focus of life in Grenada. Here, the island's bounty is apparent: on any market day, a visitor may find 28 varieties of fruit (many harvested year-round), 12 kinds of spices, and too many vegetables to count. Farm women in bright cotton dresses, aprons, and wide straw hats sit under umbrellas, tempting shoppers with bananas, papayas (called "paw-paws"), oranges, yams, plantains, melons, mangoes, breadfruit, christophines (vegetables

(continued on page 49)

SCENES OF GRENADA

▲ Large and small sailboats crowd the harbor at Carriacou, one of Grenada's islands.

➤ Brightly colored coral reefs sprawl beneath Grenada's clear blue waters.

◄ *Passengers settle in for the trip between Grenada and Carriacou.*

▼ *The white-sand beaches at Grand Anse lure tourists from throughout the world.*

▼ A bountiful variety of fresh island foods make up this Grenadian meal.

▼ A woman worker sorts nutmeg seeds, which will then be processed for export.

◀ St. George's harbor is Grenada's most important and picturesque port.

➤ Carnival, Grenada's most colorful holiday, is a time for dressing in costume.

▼ Grenada's fertile soil supports an astonishing variety of plants.

◀ 46 ▶

➤ *The open-air market in St. George's is Grenada's largest and busiest market.*

▽ *A nutmeg fruit bursts open when ripe to expose the nutmeg seed surrounded by the red fibers of mace, another spice.*

▲ *Grenadian women wash bunches of green bananas in a tub of water. Bananas have become an important Grenadian export in recent years.*

▼ *Farmers with small plots often grow extra crops to sell to neighboring islands. These farmers are packing produce on board a boat bound for Trinidad.*

◄ Most Grenadians practice Christianity, which was introduced by the Europeans.

▼ Nearly 40 percent of Grenada's population works on farms. Many Grenadians work small plots of land such as these.

(continued from page 40)

similar to potatoes), avocados, limes, callaloo greens (resembling spinach), and fresh spices. Coconut milk quenches shoppers' thirst, and fish cakes ease their appetites.

Ancient trucks laden with produce bring people to the market from the farming towns to sell their crops and shop for the week. Expert weavers ply palm fronds into hats, baskets, bags, and placemats. Women sell small, woven spice baskets filled with cinnamon, nutmeg, mace, bay leaf, vanilla, and ginger. Twenty-two kinds of fish are caught off the island's shores; the day's catch is displayed at the fish market at the Esplanade, on the oceanfront in Saint George's.

The recipes for Grenadian foods date back to the original Indian settlers, who lived off the land in the days before Columbus. Over the years, African, French, British, and East Indian influences have crept in, adding subtle flavors to the island's seafood, fruits, and vegetables. Pigeon peas (which resemble snow peas) and rice are a staple. A traditional Grenadian meal might begin with cold red pepper soup or pumpkin soup and include a fish stew or curried chicken, accompanied by a plate brimming with yams, rice and pigeon peas, and plantains—fruits that look like bananas but must be cooked before eating.

Other local dishes include roast turtle, oil down (a combination of breadfruit and salted pork steamed in coconut milk and covered with callaloo leaves), and turtle toes (ground conch, lobster, and other fish rolled into balls and deep fried). Another local dish is callaloo, a mixture of pork fat, crab, salted meat, fresh fish, okra, and callaloo greens.

Native desserts include the turtle tart (a raisin and coconut pie), coconut jelly made from the soft insides of a fresh coconut, rum cream pie, coconut ice cream smothered with island cherries, and a surprisingly tasty nutmeg, soursop, and avocado ice cream. Grenadian sweets can be sampled from pastry and fudge vendors who stroll the streets of Saint George's and Grand Anse with cloth-covered baskets.

Meals are washed down with favorite drinks: the local Carib beer; a punch of Grenadian rum, lime juice, syrup, and grated nutmeg; and

Vendors and their products fill St. George's central market during the week.

maubi, a popular drink made from the bark of the maubi tree, which Grenadians believe aids digestion. Islanders use other herbs and spices for traditional healing. They boil lime bush leaves to make tea to cure upset stomachs, and they distill mango leaves to soothe rheumatism. Some believe that plant leaves tied around the forehead can stop a fever.

Grenada's African heritage shows up not only in these folk medicine practices, but also in superstitions and belief in magic. Because of religion, education, and a higher standard of living, most Grenadians no longer believe in *duppies* (ghosts that provoke illness and disaster), zombies (walking dead), and *obeah* (an evil witchcraft). But superstition still exists on the island. The masked devils who appear in colorful costume during carnival, the annual island festival, are evidence of the pervasiveness of these beliefs. Tales of obeahman, vampires, and other horrifying creatures are the bedtime stories of the area, and people delight in hearing them.

Old legends and myths are passed down from generation to generation. Rabbits, dogs, and big cats from the jungles of Africa are powerful figures in much of the African–West Indian folklore. Animals in these tales have magical powers that allow them to assume human shapes and to frighten and outwit enemies with greater physical strength. These stories, which are entertaining and educational, are known as *anancy* tales. At Caribbean Focus 1986, a celebration of Grenadian arts and culture, islanders presented the play *Bogandeman*, based on a Grenadian anancy story. In this story, King Cat, a famous rat catcher, pretends to be dead, and rats are invited to a party to celebrate his passing. The rats are all caught and eaten with the exception of one pregnant female, which lives to continue the "rat race."

Festivals

Carnival is the highlight of the year in Grenada and throughout the Caribbean. Unlike other Caribbean countries that celebrate carnival right before Lent, Grenada celebrates in mid-August, to avoid conflict with Independence Day, February 7. At 6 A.M. on Jouvert, the first day of the festival, dancers swirl through the streets of Saint George's to the sound of steel bands and voices raised in calypso song. This day is devoted to mocking and driving out devils. Revelers disguise themselves as Jab-Jab (a Creole word derived from the French *diable*, or "devil"), streaking their faces and bodies with thick, dark grease or molasses; some carry dead snakes. Dancers pantomime their escape from hell to heaven. The following day, Grenadians dress in colorful costumes and celebrate Pretty Mas, the bright side of carnival.

Another carnival character is Short Knee, whose history tells much about the festival's origins. In the 18th century, when carnival was celebrated only by the plantation owners and their families, one of the most familiar characters was Pierrot, a clown-like entertainer with a whitened face and a loose, fancy, white dress. The Pierrot character also frequently performed at plantation house parties.

When slavery was abolished and former slaves could participate in carnival, they mimicked the Pierrot character. Beneath their long dresses they hid weapons; brawls sometimes erupted between competing bands. When the government eventually outlawed these long dresses, carnival celebrators created a new costume of brightly colored shirts with long,

An explosion of color during the grand pageant marks the end of carnival.

wide sleeves, a wire mask instead of the white face, and baggy trousers that reached just below the knee—hence the name Short Knee.

Carnival festivities include a costume parade, steel-band competitions, and the selection of a carnival queen. Calypso bands rehearse nightly to prepare for a contest held in a huge tent before a large audience. The winning calypsonian is given the title of calypso king. Carnival culminates in the grand pageant and the "jump-up," spontaneous dancing in the streets to calypso music.

The Family

In Grenadian society, the wife is considered the pillar of the family. She runs the house and looks after the children. Twenty-five years ago, couples had as many as ten children, but today the average is four or five. The smaller family size is partly the result of birth control. In addition, as the cost of living rises, more and more women work outside the home.

Three or four generations of the same family may live in the same household, forming an extended family. Child-care centers are available for the children of parents who work, but grandparents often care for the children. In turn, the elderly are generally cared for at home by their children, or they live within walking distance of their children's home.

Schoolchildren pass in front of a propaganda sign that was erected during Maurice Bishop's rule. The new government does not follow Bishop's socialist policies.

Government and Education

Grenada's leaders have often violated the nation's constitution by canceling elections, arresting political opponents, and restricting citizens' rights. The first free election since 1976, the general election of December 1984, restored a constitutional government.

Grenada is a self-governing nation associated with the Commonwealth of Nations (formerly known as the British Commonwealth). According to Grenada's constitution, the British monarch is the head of state, represented on the island by the governor-general. A native of Grenada, Sir Paul Scoon, has held this position since the country gained independence from Britain in 1974.

True power rests with the prime minister, who serves a five-year term. The prime minister oversees a cabinet of six ministers. The prime minister and cabinet make up the executive branch of the government, and they are responsible to a bicameral (two-chamber) Parliament: an upper house called the Senate and a lower house called the House of Representatives.

Grenada is divided into 15 constituencies, each of which elects a representative to a five-year term in the lower house. The representatives from the party that wins the most seats then selects the prime minister from among its ranks. The day-to-day activities of the house are presided over by the speaker of the house, who is appointed by the governor-general on the advice of the prime minister and the leader of the largest opposition party. The 13 members of the Senate are appointed; 9 are chosen by the ruling party and 4 are chosen by the opposition.

In the 1984 election, the New National party won 14 of the 15 seats in the House of Representatives and chose Herbert Blaize as prime minister. The remaining seat was won by the Grenada United Labour party, led by Sir Eric Gairy, the former head of state and Blaize's lifelong rival.

Blaize was born on Carriacou; he moved to Grenada in 1930 to attend secondary school. At one time a clerk for an American oil company in Aruba, Blaize won a seat in Grenada's colonial Parliament in 1957. In 1960, he became the island's chief minister (the colony's head of state under British rule) for 14 months, before losing an election to Gairy. When Gairy was forced out of office 18 months later, Blaize won a five-year term as chief minister. Gairy later served as Grenada's first prime minister from 1974 to 1979.

Besides the Grenada United Labour party, rival parties include the Maurice Bishop Patriotic Movement, a group loyal to the former prime minister that is led by Kendrick Radix, and the Grenada Christian Democratic Labour party, headed by Winston Whyte.

For administrative purposes, the island was originally divided into six parishes—a system of local government that was abolished during Gairy's rule. The representatives to the lower house of Parliament now handle these administrative tasks, but Prime Minister Blaize's government is working to reinstate the original parish system. The nearby islands of Carriacou and Petit Martinique have separate administrations.

Grenada's judicial system is modeled after Great Britain's. The constitution calls for the island to belong to the Eastern Caribbean Supreme Court System, which is composed of regional courts overseen by the Privy Court in England. When the New Jewel Movement was in power, Maurice Bishop abandoned the system and gave final authority over judicial matters to the Grenada Supreme Court. The Blaize government is reapplying for entry into the Eastern Caribbean system.

A governmental body appoints judges to the Supreme Court, over which Chief Justice Dennis Byron presides. The lower court system consists of local courts under the control of appointed magistrates. The island's crime rate is low; the major offense is predial larceny—the theft of garden vegetables.

The Royal Grenada Police Force, managed by an appointed police commissioner, is part of the island's security system. After the U.S. military intervention in 1983, a new police force was trained by instructors from Great Britain and Barbados to ensure that Grenada had adequate security before the foreign troops departed.

The island's fire department is organized like the police force, with an appointed fire commissioner and full-time paid firemen. The country's postal system consists of several district post offices where mail is collected. The general post office in Saint George's distributes mail throughout the island and overseas.

The Grenadian government oversees a health-care system of three general hospitals, a psychiatric hospital, and district health clinics where government-appointed doctors provide free services, including dental and prenatal care. Also, there are two private maternity hospitals on the island and three private nursing homes.

Saint George's University School of Medicine, with two campuses on the island, is an American medical school with an enrollment of between 500 and 1,000 American and Caribbean students. The school sponsors a public clinic.

The Focus on Education

Education is a high priority for the Grenadian government, and the emphasis has paid off: the adult literacy rate is estimated at 85 percent. (This means that 85 percent of adults can read and write.) Although the Ministry of Education is responsible for Grenada's public school system, the Roman Catholic church selects the teachers and runs the day-to-day school operations. Children attend primary school from ages 5 to 10 or 11,

The government places great emphasis on education, and requires compulsory attendance until age 14. Some schools, such as this one, have only meager facilities.

at which time they take the Common Entrance Exam. Students who pass this exam can enter secondary school. Those who fail must either stay in school until they are old enough for a "school-leaving" certificate or attend a junior secondary school for remedial work. After two successful years, they can continue to secondary school.

After five years of secondary school, students take a standardized test to earn their General Certificate of Exam, the equivalent of a high school diploma. After this, some students decide to attend the Institute for Further Education for two years of advanced studies, for which they earn one year of college credit.

Besides Saint George's University School of Medicine, institutions of higher education include the Grenada Teachers College and University Center, a department of the University of the West Indies.

Along with Grenada's 57 primary schools and 19 secondary schools, the island has about 60 kindergartens (both public and private) and two institutes for special education.

Job training is offered by the Grenada Technical and Vocational Institute, which is operated by the Ministry of Education. The curriculum includes training in secretarial skills, auto mechanics, drafting, refrigeration, electricity, carpentry, plumbing, and welding.

Women sort nutmeg seeds at a factory. Grenada, the world's second largest producer of nutmeg, depends on the spice for most of its export income.

Economy and Communications

Grenada is the only spice-producer in the Western Hemisphere; since the 17th century, spices have kept the nation's economy afloat. The spices grown on Grenada include nutmeg, bay leaves, allspice, cinnamon, saffron, cloves, and at least a half-dozen others.

In 1843, a local doctor named Frank Gurney introduced nutmeg to Grenada from the Portuguese East Indies. This was an important development because slavery had ended and the plantation-based sugarcane industry was beginning to decline. The newly freed slaves needed a crop they could grow on their own plots of land. Nutmeg, with its pungent aroma and spicy flavor, was the ideal crop because it flourished in the tropical climate.

Today, Grenada is the world's second largest producer of nutmeg and mace, which are the island's chief exports. In 1983, these crops earned Grenada $4.5 million. But because of the cost of processing and shipping, these spices are not tremendous money-makers. And Grenada faces strong competition from Africa and the Far East, which also grow nutmeg.

Agriculture is Grenada's largest source of export revenue. Most of the arable land—about 35,000 acres (14,000 hectares)—is used to grow nutmeg, cacao, and bananas. These three crops account for about 90 percent of Grenada's exports.

The cacao tree, from whose seeds cocoa is made, produces the largest number of seeds when it is 10 to 15 years old. After they are picked, the cacao pods are packed down to "sweat" or ferment for about a week before they are shoveled into a thin layer over canvas and laid out in the sun to dry. On most days, cacao seeds can be found drying on the quays of the harbor at Saint George's, giving the lower section of town the aroma of a vast chocolate shop. This cocoa fetches some of the highest prices on the world market.

Besides spices and cocoa, Grenadian products include coconuts, limes, and arrowroot. Some sugarcane and cotton are still grown. Fishing—chiefly by nets, trolling, and drifting with hand lines—is an important source of the country's food supply.

Tourism, the island's second largest source of income, contributes 40 percent of the gross national product. Grenadian officials expect the new Point Salines airport to increase tourism; 38,000 new visitors a year would create 1,100 new jobs for the island's workers.

Most of the tourist accommodations are small inns with 10 to 20 rooms. Grenada has only 650 hotel rooms, not enough to accommodate

A split cacao pod exposes the seeds that, when dried, are used to make cocoa.

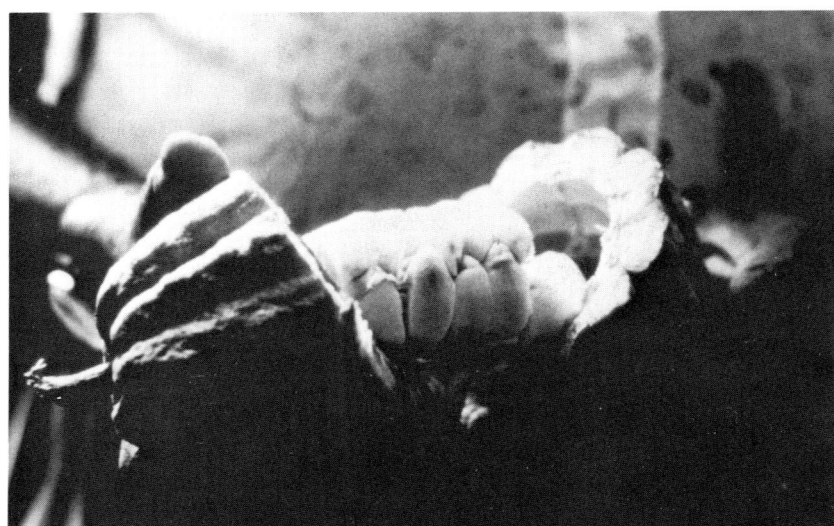

the passengers from just three jumbo jets. A master plan calls for doubling the number of hotel rooms on the island in the next three years. However, about 90 percent of Grenada's hotel rooms are located in islanders' homes, and Grenadians who want to maintain this additional income source do not favor the building of new hotels. And an unwritten law forbidding the construction of hotels taller than the island's palm trees further restricts the building of new hotels.

Grenada's industry is mainly composed of processing plants for the island's agricultural produce. These plants produce sugar, rum, soap, vegetable oils, perfume, and foodstuffs. Other industry is almost nonexistent, except for some production of furniture and clothing. The Industrial Development Corporation, founded in February 1985, is working to stimulate new industries by making it attractive for foreign companies to invest in businesses on the island. One way to do this is by offering lower tax rates for foreign corporations.

The biggest boost to Grenada's economy has come from the United States, which gave $57 million in aid for the two years after the invasion, plus $19 million to complete the Point Salines airport. This totaled $300 a year per person, among the highest rates of U.S. aid in the world. (Grenada's per capita gross domestic product is only $940.) With those funds, the inadequate road and telephone systems are under repair and new generators are being installed in the island's electrical and water systems.

Still, there are problems. Grenada is mainly rural; farming techniques are not much different from those employed 100 years ago. And when prices decline for one of its few exports, the overall earnings of Grenada plummet.

Many expected the U.S. government's aid and expertise to solve Grenada's economic problems, but the flow of money is slowing down. Now the hope is that businesses from the United States will build factories and invest in industries in order to bolster the sagging economy.

Nearly 40 percent of Grenada's 43,000-person work force earns a living through agriculture, mostly processing nutmeg, mace, and cocoa; 44

percent work in government and other services, and the rest in construction, manufacturing, and tourism. The normal workday is eight hours.

About 1,000 Grenadians are fishermen, although this is not an easy way to make a living. A day's catch brings only $1 a pound (.45 kilogram), and ice to keep the fish fresh is hard to come by. The Grenadian government provides low-interest loans to aid fishermen, but most find that they must also farm small plots of land.

Thirty percent of the labor force is unemployed. The joblessness problem is worst among young people; fully one-third are out of work. Some young men lost their jobs for refusing to join the military when Maurice Bishop was in power, and they are still unemployed. Many refuse to take available farming jobs because they are not interested in such hard labor for so little money.

Grenada's official currency is the Eastern Caribbean dollar, made up of 100 cents. Grenadians employed in agriculture earn the equivalent of U.S. $3 a day; men earn 12 percent more than women. A machine operator in the garment industry might earn $5 a day, while construction workers might earn about $20. Because groceries are inexpensive and health care is free, these salaries provide for a simple but comfortable life-style.

Grenada has a social security system to which employers and employees contribute equally. One-third of the labor force is unionized and has good benefits. Workers generally get two weeks' sick leave with full pay, and three weeks of vacation with full pay after one year; women usually get three months of maternity leave, the first two with full pay.

Transportation

Grenada's mountainous terrain makes transportation and communication difficult. There are no railroads; Grenadians must depend on the 650 miles (1,047 kilometers) of roads, most blacktop but some gravel, to travel from place to place. These narrow roads wind up and down foliage-covered mountains and curve sharply around the contours of the coast. To make matters worse, many of the roads are in poor condition. The Bishop

Grenadian women watch an American-built road-paving machine at work. The United States has helped rebuild and repair much of Grenada's road system.

government added 45 miles (73 km) of desperately needed new roads, but some of these were destroyed during the U.S. invasion. The U.S. aid package included funds for upgrading and rebuilding highways, and a coastal road network should be completed by the end of 1987.

Fewer than half of the islanders own automobiles; some have old-model cars, and others drive mini-mokes—open, jeeplike vehicles that use little gas, which costs about $2.50 a gallon (3.79 liters). Most Grenadians depend on low-priced local buses for transportation. Buses leave for almost every town and village from Market Square in Saint George's. Taxis are plentiful in the tourist areas, and drivers often double as tour guides.

The Port Salines International Airport, which opened in October 1984, allows large commercial jets to land on Grenada. British West Indies Air provides daily flights from Miami; along with Grenada Airways, it also flies nonstop once a week from New York. Other major airlines have flights to Barbados that connect with Leeward Islands Air Transport to Grenada. More international airlines will probably establish direct passenger service to Grenada.

The island of Carriacou can be reached by interisland schooner or Leeward Islands Air Transport from Grenada. Petit Martinique can be reached only by boat from Carriacou.

Saint George's is regarded as the most picturesque port in the Caribbean. North American cruise lines and freighters from around the world regularly make this a port of call. Berths for two oceangoing vessels with lengths of 400 to 500 feet (120 to 150 meters) are available alongside an 800-foot (240-m) pier. No tugboats are necessary. Fishing boats congregate in the well-sheltered natural harbor.

Communicating the News

Leslie Pierre founded the *Grenadian Voice* newspaper in 1981 as an independent alternative to Maurice Bishop's official government newspaper, the *Free West Indian*. Pierre was arrested for starting a newspaper without government authorization after he sold 3,000 copies of the first issue. A month after the U.S. invasion, Pierre published the second issue of the *Voice*. Today, his *Grenadian Voice* is the main newspaper on the island. Published weekly, it is a general-interest publication covering local news, sports, arts, and business. Other papers include the *Indies Times*, privately published by followers of Bishop, and the *National*, run by the ruling New National party.

The island's only radio station, state-owned Radio Grenada, broadcasts a wide range of programs, including local and regional news, news from the British Broadcasting Corporation, sports roundups, interviews, educational programs, and West Indian music.

Only about 7 percent of Grenadians have television sets. The island's first television station, built by the Cubans during Maurice Bishop's rule, was destroyed during the U.S. invasion. In November 1985, a new television station built with private American aid began broadcasting. The station, which is called Discovery Television, is on the air about three to four hours a day, showing local news broadcasts, sports, entertainment (carnival is well covered), and family-oriented programming from the U.S.-based Christian Broadcasting Network.

Small fishing and passenger boats lie at anchor in the harbor at St. George's. The hilly, beautiful city is the island's largest and the nation's capital.

Saint George's and Other Cities

Grenada's capital and hub of commercial and intellectual life is Saint George's, which lies on a natural harbor that is actually the crater of an extinct volcano. Originally called Fort Royale, the city was founded in 1705 by the French governor of Grenada. In 1763, the English occupied the city and renamed it Saint George's in honor of King George III.

The French and British influences are readily seen in the capital's buildings. French architectural details, such as ornate wrought-iron work, survive among British Georgian-West Indian buildings with their mellowed bricks and red tiles. Wood has been a forbidden building material since a number of disastrous fires occurred in the settlement's early years, so most buildings are built of brick that was brought over as ballast on British trading ships.

Pastel-painted warehouses, many built in the 18th century, cling to the curving shore along the inner harbor. The steep green hills behind the harbor are lined with neat, rainbow-colored houses with red and green shingled roofs.

Saint George's is the hilliest city in the Caribbean—and one of the most beautiful. The town is divided in half by a high ridge, and the Sendall Tunnel allows passage between the two areas. The western side of town is the site of the open-air market; the eastern side is known as the Carenage

The Gothic architecture of centuries-old churches graces St. George's.

area. Commercial activity dominates the main street, which wraps itself around the horseshoe-shaped harbor. Fishing boats, many constructed by shipwrights in the Grenadines, dock here. On Tuesday afternoons, crates of fruits and vegetables bound for Trinidad are loaded aboard cargo boats.

The Grenada National Museum, under the direction of the Grenada Historical Society, is housed in a former French army garrison and prison built in 1704. The museum has a collection of ancient Indian pottery and colonial artifacts, and there are finds from archaeological digs, including Indian rock carvings known as petroglyphs.

Centuries-old churches that combine soft West Indian pastels with traditional European architecture sit on high ridges ringing the capital. The pink, 19th-century Anglican church with its beautiful stained-glass windows is lined with stone memorial tablets carved in England and dedicated to British soldiers who fought against the French. The clock tower atop Saint Andrew's Presbyterian Church, built in 1830, is a landmark of Saint George's skyline.

The coastal road north from Saint George's winds past mountains and valleys covered with banana and breadfruit trees, palms, bamboo, and tropical flowers. About a half-hour drive north of Saint George's is the village of Gouyave. The weathered, red-roofed houses strung along the sea wall are dominated by Anglican and Catholic churches. Gouyave is a fishing center and the home of the west coast spice-processing industry. At Dougaldston Estate, near the entrance of town, cloves, cinnamon, mace, nutmeg, allspice, and cacao are laid out on giant trays to dry in the sun. Barefoot women walk through the spices to dry them evenly. They sort and grade them by hand, much as they have done for more than 100 years.

Along the east coast lies Westerhall, the so-called Beverly Hills of Grenada, known for its beautiful villas, gardens, and views. The inland route back to Saint George's cuts through the mountains, past hundreds of small farms. The road winds upward through the rain forest, then back down into the sun.

There are no fast-food chains, high-rise hotels, gambling, or dusk-to-dawn nightlife on the island, and most Grenadians intend to keep it that way. Still, modern times and technology are slowly changing the Grenadian way of life.

A woman dances to the rhythmic music of a steel-drum band. The steel drum is only one of the instruments used to make the music heard throughout Grenada.

Arts and Culture

Grenada's music has a long history. It has been strongly influenced by African musical styles, although European elements have fused with it. Calypso, a combination of singing and dancing, is heard throughout the country, particularly at carnival time. Its origins are not documented, but the most frequently told story is that calypso began with West Indian slaves who were forbidden to talk to one another. But because they were permitted to sing, the workers communicated through personalized songs, using a slang that their masters could not understand.

Calypso singers improvise rhyming commentaries on love, politics, personalities, and controversial current events. The lyrics, often humorous and sexy, sometimes insulting, are sung to a melodic African beat. American rap music draws upon the calypso tradition.

Calypsonians write their own lyrics and melodies and give themselves nicknames, such as Grenada's Mighty Scaramouche and Black Wizard. Sophisticated calypso bands use electric guitars, accordians, string basses, and maracas. The primitive variety, called scratch bands, are trios whose members play a flute, a long bamboo pipe, and a gourd that is carved so that when it is scratched, it produces a sound similar to mandolin music.

Jump-up, spirited dancing in the streets to calypso music, is part of the carnival festivities. Grenadians also do the limbo, an acrobatic West

African tribal dance said to imitate the movements of an imprisoned slave wriggling toward freedom. As drums beat, a dancer arches underneath a long bar that is lowered after each successful pass.

Steel-drum music, which originated in Trinidad, is a popular form of entertainment. Most steel bands use sawed-off oil drums, whose tops are hammered to produce different pitches. Other bands use parts from junked automobiles.

Musicians use a variety of other instruments, including the maruga and maraca, which are of native Indian origin; rhythm instruments, such as drums, marimbas, banjos, and *palitos* from Africa; and accordions, saxophones, flutes, and other wind instruments from Europe.

The Grenadian government actively encourages the island's diverse cultural groups with events such as the 1985 Grenada Festival of the Arts. Several folk groups also perform traditional music. The Cariawa Folk Group, from the parish of Saint Patrick's, specializes in singing and choreographing folk songs, especially those in the Grenadian patois. The Concord Folk Group wants to revive interest in Grenadian-style social dances, such as lancers and quadrilles, and uses native instruments like the cocolute. The Tamarind Folk Group has researched the folk dances of Grenada and choreographed them for stage performances. The National Folk Group, made up of members from six of the island's most accomplished cultural groups, was formed in 1985 to give foreigners an insight into aspects of Grenadian folk life through musical performances. The Marryshow Folk Theater in Saint George's is Grenada's first cultural center; it features folk theater, West Indian dance and music, and poetry readings by local groups. Cultural troupes from Barbados and Trinidad perform here as well.

Grenada's literary tradition dates from the 1920s and 1930s, when island writers first began to deal with the realities of Caribbean life. The history of slavery and colonialism made social protest a natural and frequent theme. Authors often used humor, even when describing poor social conditions and prejudices.

Three young boys sit with a model sailboat they have carved from wood. Grenada's wood carvers are renowned for their skill.

Wilfred Redhead is one of Grenada's leading authors. Several of his one-act plays have been performed throughout the Caribbean, and a number of his short stories have been aired over the British Broadcasting Corporation radio service. His latest book, *A City on a Hill*, recounts his memories of early Saint George's.

In 1944, the country of Haiti popularized the style of painting known as naive. Also called "primitive" or "grass-roots," naive painting uses vivid colors and simple outlines to depict a wide range of subjects from everyday life. This style spread throughout the Caribbean and is particularly popular in Grenada.

Most Grenadian painters and sculptors are self-taught artists. Painters generally represent what they know best—regattas, fishing activities, fruit

A Grenadian woman displays one of her paintings. Local artists often paint scenes that reflect the island's relationship with the sea.

gathering, landscapes, and scenes of Saint George's harbor. Sculptors are inspired by the island's plants and animals, folk dancers, and drummers.

Native painter Elinus Cato is one of the island's finest artists; his work has represented Grenada at several international exhibitions, including shows in London and Washington, D.C. He paints countryside and town scenes in bright reds, greens, yellows, and blues. Cato, who avoids social or political themes, is a master at depicting the charm and warmth of the Grenadian people. His *People at Work* was selected as a gift for Queen Elizabeth II when she visited the island in 1985.

Canute Caliste is another extremely popular and prolific artist, producing 60 or more paintings a year. A violinist and the father of 20, he lives on Carriacou in a house by the sea. He paints happy scenes of Carriacou-style weddings, carnival bands, jump-ups, regattas, boat-launching fêtes, and big drum dances.

Grenadian sculptors carve beautiful local wood—mahogany, teak, saman, blue mahoe, eucalyptus—into two- and three-dimensional works. Among the most outstanding are Alexander Alexis, John Pivott, and Stanley Coutain, who was commissioned to carve the frame for Cato's painting for Queen Elizabeth II.

Grenadian handicrafts began with the early settlement of the island by Indians from South America. Excavations at Point Salines, Duquesne Bay, and Sauteurs have uncovered finely crafted terra-cotta cooking pots and ceremonial vessels, intricately carved sculptures, arrowheads, and stone carvings called petroglyphs.

The local handicraft industry is thriving, thanks to the Grenada National Institute of Handicrafts production and training center. Crafts sold at the institute's retail outlet are made from materials grown on the island. Straw, bamboo, and wicker are used to weave hats, bags, and purses. Furniture, kitchen utensils, and salad bowls are carved from mahogany and red cedar. Craftsmen also fashion jewelry of black coral and turtleshell.

Grenadians hope that the opening of a new international airport will increase the flow of tourists to the island's pleasant and inviting beaches.

Looking to the Future

Grenadians are optimistic about the future of their island. Aid from the United States is being used to rebuild roads and improve power and communications systems. Jumbo jets can now land at Point Salines International Airport, bringing tourists directly to the island. A free press is operating with the publication of the *Grenadian Voice*, a privately run newspaper that was suppressed by Maurice Bishop.

In 1984, in the first free general election since 1976, moderate candidate Herbert A. Blaize was elected prime minister. However, when Blaize's five-year term expires in 1989, the island's political future will be open once again. A good number of Grenadians are still loyal to Sir Eric Gairy, who has returned to Grenada. There is a small group of former followers of the New Jewel Movement who support the Maurice Bishop Patriotic Movement.

Despite some changes for the better, problems persist: about 30 percent of the people are unemployed, there is little income from foreign investment, and communications and transportation between cities and towns are poor. The main pillars of Grenada's economy—agriculture and tourism—are unstable. Nutmeg, cocoa, and bananas, Grenada's main exports, are suffering from low world prices and bad harvests during the Bishop regime. Recovery is hard to predict; like many small island nations,

Grenada is economically dependent on the changing forces of international trade.

Local businessmen are counting heavily on the Point Salines airport to revive the economy, especially tourism, which until now depended mainly on visits by cruise ships. But more tourists require more hotels, which must be quickly built in order to house them.

Because of its richness in spices and its strategic location, the tiny island of Grenada may always be a pawn in a chess game between more powerful nations. In the long match between France and Great Britain, the British won. Now the United States wants to make Grenada a model for the Eastern Caribbean, with a healthy business community and pro-American political parties. "It's sad," a former official in the Bishop government has said. "The majority of Grenadians never intended to become this bone of contention between East and West."

Alister Hughes, editor of the *Grenada Newsletter*, warned that "Grenada and the United States must exercise great skill in striking a careful balance that will promote our development without smothering us under a blanket of dollar bills." Some islanders fear that as the United States tries to prove itself with economic aid, they will lose their distinctive characteristics as West Indians.

Although Grenada's future is uncertain, there are some constants, if four centuries of history hold true. The temperature will hover at a comfortable 80° Fahrenheit (27° Centigrade) year-round. The fertile soil will yield a bounty of exotic spices, fruits, and vegetables. The islanders will continue to value close-knit families, education, and religion. And the independent spirit of the Grenadian people will triumph—as it always has.

GLOSSARY

Anancy tales	Island folk stories that feature animals with magical powers and are entertaining and educational.
Cacao	A tree whose seeds are used to make cocoa and chocolate. It is one of the three chief crops of Grenada.
Callaloo	Greens similar to spinach that are used in several Grenadian recipes. Also a dish that contains callaloo greens, pork fat, crab, salted meat, fresh fish, and okra.
Calypso	The distinctive music of the West Indies, based on African rhythms and influenced by European and American dance music. Many calypso songs are spontaneous commentaries on current events or local personalities.
Caribbean Andes	A partially submerged mountain chain that once connected North and South America. The islands of the West Indies are the mountaintops of the Caribbean Andes.
Carnival	An annual festival celebrated in most Caribbean countries, usually before Lent.
Christophine	A vegetable similar to a potato.
Duppies	In island folklore, ghosts that provoke illness or disaster.
Guayabera	A lightweight shirt-jacket worn by most Grenadian men.
Jab-Jab	From the French *diable*, or "devil." The Jab-Jab, a disguise worn by many Grenadians during carnivals,

	involves painting the face with dark grease or molasses and sometimes carrying a dead snake.
Jump-up	Lively dancing in the streets to calypso music that is part of the carnival festivities.
Lesser Antilles	The chain of Caribbean islands that runs from the Virgin Islands in the north to Grenada in the south. They are generally small. The northern Lesser Antilles are also called the Leeward Islands; the southern Lesser Antilles are the Windward Islands.
Limbo	A West Indian dance in which the dancer wriggles under a horizontal pole. The pole is lowered for each dancer. Some people say that the limbo was originally a West African tribal dance that resembled the movements of a slave wriggling toward freedom.
Mace	A spice made from the processed fibers that coat the seeds of the nutmeg plant.
Marxism	Political, economic, and social views based on the writings of the 19th-century German philosopher Karl Marx. Marx advocated leadership by the workers with the eventual goal of a classless society.
Maubi	A drink made from the bark of the maubi tree and believed to aid digestion.
Mongoose Gang	A secret police force that operated under Prime Minister Eric Gairy during the 1970s. It was accused of harassment of Gairy's opponents and the murder of members of the rival New Jewel Movement.
Obeah	Evil witchcraft, related to the voodoo practices of other Caribbean islands. Obeah and other forms of voodoo originated in African tribal beliefs and rituals brought to the New World by slaves.
Oil down	An island dish consisting of breadfruit and salted pork steamed in coconut milk and covered with callaloo greens.
Predial larceny	The theft of garden vegetables—Grenada's most common crime.

Radical	A member of a political party or group who takes extreme positions on political issues.
Scratch bands	Simple calypso bands whose members play a flute, a bamboo pipe, and a carved gourd that makes twanging sounds when scratched.
Zombies	According to obeah superstition, zombies are dead people brought back to life to serve the voodoo leaders. Some so-called zombies may actually have been dosed with poisonous drugs to make them appear corpselike and forget their identities.

INDEX

A
Abercromby, Sir Ralph 28
allspice 10, 61
American Indians 39
anancy tales 51, 81
Annandale Falls 22
Antigua 30, 35
Arawak Indians 11, 27
arrowroot 10, 62
Aruba 56
Atlantic Ocean 15, 19, 27
Austin, Hudson 12, 34–36

B
Bacelot Bay 22
Bahamas 19
bananas 10, 21, 40, 49, 61, 79
Barbados 19, 30, 35, 57, 74
bay leaves 10, 61
Belle Vue North 23
Belle Vue South 23
Bishop, Maurice 12, 17, 31–35, 56, 64, 66, 67, 79, 80
Bishop, Rupert 31, 32
Black Bay River 9, 22
Black Power movement 32
Blaize, Herbert 12, 37, 56, 79
Bloody Monday 31
Bloody Wednesday 34
Bloody Sunday 31
Bogandeman 51

Braithwaite, Nicholas 36
British Commonwealth 10, 55
Byron, Dennis 57

C
cacao 10, 61, 62, 63, 79, 81
Caliste, Canute 76
Calivigny Island 22
callaloo greens 40, 49, 81
calypso 52, 73, 81
Canada 33
Carenage 69
Caribbean Andes 19, 81
Caribbean Community 10
Caribbean Islands 11, 36, 69, 75
Caribbean Sea 15
Carib Indians 11, 16, 27, 28, 39
carnival 51, 52, 73, 81
Carriacou 22, 56, 66, 76
Carter, Jimmy 33
Castro, Fidel 33, 35
Cato, Elinus 76
Christian Democratic Labour party 56
Christophine 40, 81
Ciboney Indians 11, 27
cinnamon 10, 15, 40, 61
Clarke Court Bay 22
cloves 10, 15, 61
Coard, Bernard 12, 17, 33–36
cocoa *(see* cacao)

coconuts 10, 62
Columbus, Christopher 11, 16, 27, 49
Common Entrance Exam 58
Commonwealth of Nations 10, 17, 55
Comte d'Estaing 11
Concord Valley 22
Concord Waterfall 22
cotton 10, 23
Creft, Jacqueline 34
Cuba 12, 17, 19, 30, 32, 33, 35

D

de Cerrillac, Comte Jean Faudoas 11, 28
Dominica 30, 35
du Parquet, Jean-Marie Bonnard 28
duppies 50, 81
Duquesne River 9, 21, 76

E

Eastern Caribbean Dollar 64
Eastern Caribbean Supreme Court System 56
Emanicipation Act 12, 28
Esplanade 49

F

Federation of the West Indies 10, 30
Fedon, Julien 12, 28
Florida 19
Free West Indian 66
Fort Frederick 11, 28
Fort Royale 69
Fort Rupert 11, 28, 34
France 16

G

Gairy, Sir Eric 12, 17, 31, 32, 56, 79
General Certificate of Exam 58
Glover Island 22

Gouyave 9
Government House 36
Grand Anse Bay 22, 40, 49
Grand Etang Lake 9, 20, 21, 24
Great Britain 16, 30, 56, 57, 80
Greater Antilles 19
Great River Valley 21
Green Island 22
Grenada Festival of the Arts 74
Grenada Supreme Court 56
Grenada United Labor party 12, 31, 56
Grenadian Voice 66, 79
Grenadine Islands 15, 23
Grenville 9, 21, 22, 40
Gun Point 23

H

Haiti 75
Hillsborough 23
Hog Island 22
House of Representatives 10, 55, 56
Hughes, Alister 80
Hurricane Janet 12, 25

I

Indies News 66
Ronde Island 23
Institute for Further Education 58

J

Jab-Jab 51, 81
Jamaica 30, 35
Jump-up 51, 52, 73, 82

L

La Grenade 11
Lake Antoine 9, 20
L'Anse aux Épines 22, 40
Leeward Islands 19, 30
Lesser Antilles 19, 28, 82

Levera Bay 22
Levera Beach 22
Levera Pond 9, 20
limes 10, 23, 49, 62
Little Saint Patrick River 9, 21

M
Market Square 34, 65
Martinique 11, 28
maubi 50, 82
Maurice Bishop Patriotic Movement 56, 79
Ministry of Education 57
Mongoose Gang 31, 82
Montserrat 35
Morne Rouge 40
Mount Granby 21
Mount Lebanon 21
Mount Saint Catherine 9, 21
Mount Sinai 21

N
National 66
New Jewel Movement (NJM) 12, 17, 31, 35, 56, 79
New National party 56, 66
nutmeg 10, 15, 49, 61, 63, 79

O
obeah 31, 50, 82
Operation Urgent Fury 36
Organization of American States 10
Organization of East Caribbean States 10, 17, 35

P
patois 39
Pearls Airport 33
People at Work 76

People's Revolutionary Government 12, 31, 32
Petit Martinique 15, 23, 24, 56, 66
Pierre, Leslie 66
Point Salines 17, 20, 33, 62, 63, 66, 76, 79, 80
Pretty Mas 51

R
Radio Grenada 66
Radix, Kendrick 56
Reagan, Ronald 17, 33, 36
Redhead, Wilfred 75
Revolutionary Military Council 35
Richmond Hill Prison 36

S
saffron 10, 61
Saint George's 9, 21, 22, 28, 34, 36, 39, 40, 49, 51, 57, 62, 65, 66, 69, 75, 76
Saint John's River 21
Saint Kitts 29, 35
Saint Lucia 29, 35
Saint Vincent 19, 22, 23, 30, 35
Sandy Island 22
Sans Souci 40
Sauteurs 9, 76
Sauteurs Bay 20
Scoon, Sir Paul 12, 17, 30, 36, 55
Senate 10, 55
Sendall Tunnel 69
Soviet Union 17, 32, 33, 36
sugar 10
Sugar Loaf 22

T
Tobago 30
Treaty of Versailles 12, 28

Trinidad 19, 28, 30, 74
Tyrrel Bay 23, 24

U
United Nations 10
United States 17, 33, 35–37, 63, 65, 79, 80

V
vampires 50
Venezuela 15, 19
Virgin Islands 19

W
West Indian Associated States 12, 30
West Indies 15, 19, 24
Whyte, Winston 56
Windward Islands 15, 19, 30

Z
zombies 50, 83

PICTURE CREDITS
AP/Wide World Photos (pp. 34, 37, 38, 54); Bettman Newsphotos (pp. 65); Carolina Biological Supply Company (pp. 42–43); Compix (pp. 47 below); Defense Department (pp. 35); Grenada Tourist Department (title page; pp. 18, 20–21, 41, 43 (below), 44 (above), 44 (below), 44–45, 45 (above), 45 (below), 46 (above), 46 (below), 47 (above), 50, 52, 60, 62, 68, 70, 72, 75, 78); Dr. Donald L. Hill (cover; pp. 14, 16, 24, 42, 43 (above), 58, 76); Library of Congress (pp. 26, 29); United Nations pp. 30).